DAD AND THE DUCKS

DR. LURIELA CLEMENTE

ILLUSTRATED BY CARMEN MASTERSON

About the Author

Dr. Clemente has been an elementary educator for 25 years. She desires to inspire children's imagination and a love for reading.

DEDICATION

This book is dedicated to my two young grandchildren:
Roman and Eliana. I hope to contribute to their love of
reading. To my husband, thank you for believing in me. To
my daughter Carmen, thank you for illustrating my dream.

"Look at what I brought!" Dad said excitedly while holding a cardboard box from which some suspicious sounds could be heard.

The children and Mom curiously gathered around
Dad as he revealed what surprise was chirping from
inside the box.

The children squealed with joy when they saw the three little mallard ducklings.

"Duckies!" they exclaimed.

Mom was not as impressed with the surprise.
"Why would we want ducks?" she asked.

"Where are we going to put them? Who is going to
feed them? Who is cleaning after them?" Mom did
not look pleased.

Dad kissed Mom on the cheek and told her,
"But… I love you!" As the children crowded around
the ducks, Mom realized this was not an argument
she would win.

Dad set the ducks up comfortably on the back porch, and the adventure began.

Dad knew that mallards love to swim, so he filled a tub in the backyard with water and let the ducks take a bath. The ducks zipped back and forth under the water, splashing around, as the kids looked on.

A new routine had started! The family loved caring after the ducklings. The children couldn't wait to come back from school to play with them.

Dad fed them. Mom cleaned up after them.

Dad taught the ducklings to go on walks. The three mallard ducklings followed Dad in a single file. He was their Mama Duck!

The kids took turns helping Dad lead the line of
clumsy ducks.

But mallards need to learn to fly too! It is part of growing up! Since Dad was now honorary Mama Duck, he decided to teach them to fly.

He tossed the ducks in the air for a few minutes each day. The ducks flapped their wings and crashed back down a few steps ahead. It took days of practice, but the ducks were finally getting stronger and flying a bit further.

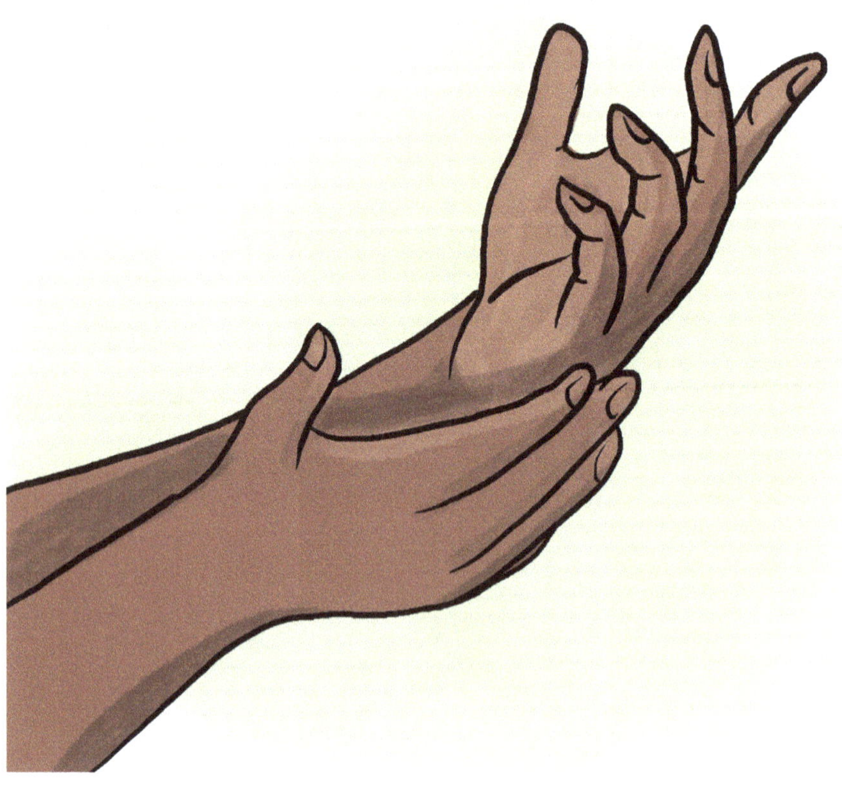

One day, the ducks took off and flew above a few houses, then they turned around and came back, but... they didn't know how to land!

They landed on the roof of the family's house and honked down to the family, desperately asking for help. Dad had to climb onto the roof and bring them down one by one.

The children couldn't contain their laughter at
watching Dad rescue the ducklings.

After more weeks of practice, the ducks had the
confidence to try flying higher than they ever had.
They flew a circle around the neighborhood, and
once they were above the family again, honked down
as if to say "Goodbye, family!"

The family waited and waited, but the ducks did not
come back.

The children were so sad, they missed the ducks so much! They worried they wouldn't have anything to eat! Where would they sleep?

Dad and Mom sat down with them and explained that mallard ducks are meant to be free and fly wherever they wanted.

Dad told them that he never meant for the ducks to live with them forever, they needed to be set free. The children wanted the ducklings to stay little forever, but alas, all creatures eventually grow up.

Life went on and the children still talked wistfully about the ducks, but one day about a year later…

Surprise!! The ducks came back to visit their old home! This time, to introduce their own little ducklings to their old family!

THE END

www.ingramcontent.com/pod-product-compliance
Lightning Source LLC
Chambersburg PA
CBHW041146300726
48978CB00016B/1399